GIRLS' CAMP

AN EROTIC ADVENTURE

VICTORIA RUSH

VOLUME 7

JADE'S EROTIC ADVENTURES - BOOK 7

COPYRIGHT

THE HABIT

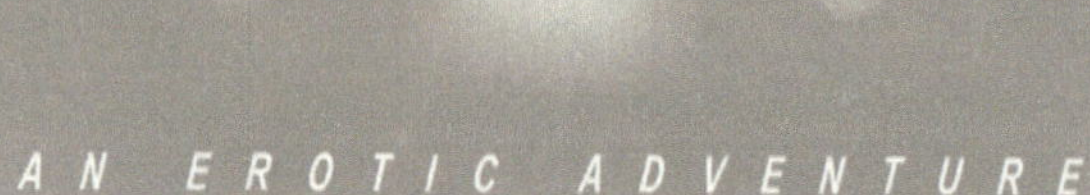

VICTORIA RUSH

Some habits are harder to break than others...

Artificial intelligence never felt so real...

Feeling the burn never felt so good...

Books 6 - 10 in the bestselling series - now 60% off.

For the uninhibited...

1

———

FALLING FOR THE GIRL

I woke to the sound of my phone rattling on the nightstand. I ignored it for a few seconds, then buried my head under my pillow, squeezing the sides trying to muffle the noise. For the last week or so, I'd had more trouble than usual getting my day started. After the girl next door had gone off to college, I felt hopelessly alone and depressed. Even though our affair only lasted a couple of weeks, it had injected an exciting spark into my love life that had been missing for far too long. Now I was all alone again, with only my freelance graphic design job giving me any reason to get out of bed in the morning.

After a few minutes, the phone started buzzing again, and I rolled over to glance at the screen. It was an incoming call from my best friend, Hannah. Normally, she texted me at this time of the day, so it must have been important. I reached over and tapped the speaker button, then flopped back down on the bed.

"Hello?" I said, groggily.

"Are you *still* not up?" Hannah said. "I'm getting worried

about you, girl. You haven't set foot out of your place for over two weeks."

"Welcome to the life of a lonely freelance artist. Sometimes I wonder if it was such a good idea quitting the firm. At least you see some familiar faces every day."

"You haven't been answering my texts lately."

"I've been...*busy*."

"Sleeping in and feeling sorry for yourself?"

I paused, thinking how best to respond. I hadn't told Hannah about my recent fling with the girl next door.

"Something like that."

"Listen," she said. "I've been thinking. Summer's almost over. We need to get you out of the house and get your circulation pumping again. Me and some of the girls from the office were thinking of taking a camping trip."

"What, to Yosemite again?"

"Even better. *Canada.* Lilly knows a quiet place way up north that's hardly been touched by human civilization. We can go full-on commando. Portage in by canoe, catch our own fish, go skinny dipping—the whole nine yards. It'll be good for you to get away for a while. Just you and me and four other girls."

The idea of swimming in the nude with people I knew made me feel a bit uncomfortable. I still hadn't come out with Hannah or anyone else about my recent lesbian dalliances.

"Skinny dipping? Won't it be *cold* up there? That doesn't sound like my idea of relaxing."

"The lakes are small and shallow, not like Lake Michigan. They get super-warm this time of the year. Plus, they're crystal clear and utterly pristine. Lilly says you can actually *drink* from them. When was the last time you felt comfortable doing that?"

I glanced out my window toward Abby's house and sighed.

"I don't know, Han..."

"Well I'm not letting you off the hook this time," Hannah said. "We've already booked the tickets. We fly into Toronto Wednesday morning, drive a rental car north for a few hours, then arrive back home middle of next week. Your freelance business can survive without your attention for a week."

"What—no laptops? Do they have cell reception up there?"

"No, and no. The only thing you're allowed to pack that has any kind of battery is your vibrator. But we'll be too busy having other kinds of fun to think about sex. Building campfires, roasting marshmallows, running away from bears—"

"Bears?"

"Just kidding. They do have black bears in that neck of the woods, but Lilly says as long as we keep a clean campsite, they'll leave us alone. Are you in?"

I rolled over and pulled my duvet over my shoulders.

"Arghh. I suppose so. As long as I can bring my comforter with me."

"No way," Hannah said. "We have to pack light, just the necessities. We're going to be carrying everything in and out on our back, including the canoes. Three tents, some air mattresses, sleeping bags, and a minimum of provisions. We'll catch everything else we need."

"Fine. As long as I don't have to clean the fish."

Hannah chuckled.

"Lilly's our designated cook. She grew up not far from where we're going. She'll show us how to catch, clean, and cook everything."

Hannah paused for a moment over the line.

"Are you going to be able to drag yourself out of bed at five a.m. this Wednesday to catch the early flight?"

"Go away!" I said, pulling the comforter over my head. "I'll call you later today to finalize the arrangements."

"Atta girl. You're gonna love this. The sky is so clear at night, it practically looks like cream, there are so many stars. It'll be just us girls and the cry of the loon over the still water."

"And bears. Don't forget about the bears."

E arly Wednesday morning, Hannah picked me up at my place and we drove to O'Hare airport together. She was excited about the trip, but I was still having second thoughts about going away with so many people I knew. No one yet knew about my recent lesbian experiences—not even Hannah—and I wasn't sure if I'd be able to hide my attraction to six scantily-clad women alone in the wilderness.

"You've been awfully quiet lately," she said, glancing at me watching the cars go by.

"I've just been doing a lot of thinking lately. You know, after the divorce, it's been a little...strange. Not knowing what to do with myself, not having anybody to share intimate moments with..."

"Well nothing's going to happen staying holed up alone in your house, that's for sure. You've got to get back on the horse. I've been trying to take you out to the bar for quite a while now—"

I shook my head and sighed.

"That's just not my scene anymore, Han. I'm getting too...*old* for those pick-up routines."

Hannah took her eyes off the road for a moment and stared at me.

"But you still like *men*, right? I hope you haven't lost your mojo. You're just reaching your sexual prime—"

"It's still there. I guess I'm just looking for the...right one."

"Well let's not worry about any of that for a few days. It's just going to be us girls in the middle of nowhere, with no one around for miles. We don't need no stinking men where we're going!"

I huffed an awkward chuckle, then looked out my window at the passing traffic.

———

The drive north from Toronto into the Canadian interior was stunning. I marveled at all the pretty rivers and lakes alongside the highway, dotted with pretty boathouses and motor yachts plying the dark blue water. The landscape got increasingly rugged the further we got from the city, and about halfway to our final destination we stopped at an outfitter's to rent two canoes. We chose the top-of-the-line skiffs made of fiberglass and kevlar, and I was surprised how easy it was to lift them up and strap them to the top of our big SUV.

Lilly sat up front while Hannah provided navigation using a crumpled old map from her childhood. Bonnie and Madison, who I already knew from my previous job, sat in the middle seat, while I sat in the rear jumper seat with the new girl, Emma. It was hard keeping my attention focused on the passing scenery with her downy legs poking through skimpy cargo shorts rubbing against me on the cramped bench.

She was a little younger than the rest of us, somewhere

in her late twenties I estimated, but absolutely gorgeous. Long corkscrew-curly hair tumbled over her plump youthful cheeks and pretty rosebud lips. She reminded me of the college girl Abby, and I kept stealing glances at her exposed legs whenever she peered out her window.

"Everything okay back there?" Hannah called from the front seat, peering into the rearview mirror. "Jade, are you and Emma getting caught up? You're the only ones who don't really know each other. I hope you guys are making friends—we've got a long trip ahead of us."

"Emma's a doll," I said, stealing another quick glance at her. "We've been pointing out our favorite boathouses along the way. This really is God's country up here."

"You haven't seen anything yet," Lilly said, from the front seat. "What 'til you get to Algonquin Park. It's even *more* beautiful up there. No boats, no cars, and no people. Just the quietest, most serene lake country you'll ever experience."

"How did you know about this place?" Madison chimed in from the middle seat.

"My grandparents had a cottage on Lake Muskoka, not too far from here. I used to spend every summer there growing up, waterskiing during the day, lying on the dock to get a tan, entertaining friends at night. My granddad was the one who taught me how to fish. There's nothing like the taste of fresh-caught smallmouth bass cooked in a skillet with nothing but butter. You guys are going to die and thought you'd gone to heaven."

"If I don't die first watching you cut its head off," I joked.

The last few miles to our embarkation point took us along a narrow gravel road through thick maple and birch trees. We could hear the overhanging branches scraping against the hulls of the overturned canoes on the roof of our car, and I smiled at Emma when she reached over and grasped my hand in excitement. The road terminated in a thicket by a small parking lot, and we locked our car near a beat-up old Pathfinder, then lifted our heavy backpacks loaded with provisions onto our shoulders.

Lilly and Hannah took the lead carrying the first canoe, while Bonnie and Madison followed close behind carrying the second one. Emma and I took up the rear, keeping a nervous watch out for bears. The trail was narrow and rough, with plenty of dips and boulders to navigate. I was glad I'd brought my hiking shoes as I stepped gingerly over the slippery moss-covered rocks.

"Are we there yet?" I called ahead to Hannah and Lilly, only half-kidding.

"It's about thirty more minutes to the main lake where we'll put in," Lilly said. "But there's a pretty waterfall about halfway where we can rest and freshen up."

"Suck it up, trooper," Hannah said. "Don't be a pussy. We haven't even got to the hard part yet. Enjoy the scenery. Can't you smell the fresh scent of the Great White North?"

"I thought that was the scent of your stinky armpits," I joked.

Fifteen minutes later, we began to hear the distant sound of a waterfall as the trail began to get steeper and more treacherous. The girls carrying the canoes had to walk carefully so as not to lose their footing and topple the canoes from their shoulders. I suddenly felt guilty about not carrying my weight.

"Do you guys need a third?" I shouted ahead. "Those canoes look pretty heavy. I'm happy to lend another shoulder."

"It's actually easier to maneuver with two than three," Lilly said. "But after our rest stop, I'll be happy to switch if you're still game. It's getting a bit hot under here. I could use some fresh air."

The sound of falling water grew louder and louder until we came upon a small, sloped waterfall at the side of our trail.

"Let's stop here and cool off for a bit," Lilly said. "Do you guys feel like a refreshing shower?"

"Hell, yes!" Hannah said, as she and Lilly lifted the canoe off their shoulders and lowered it to the ground.

I looked at everybody's cargo pants, fleece vests, and heavy hiking boots.

"Aren't we a little overdressed?" I said.

"It's just us girls out here," Hannah replied, beginning to strip off her outerwear. "Who needs clothes?"

She and Lilly stripped down to their bra and panties, then they paused and looked at the rest of us playfully.

"Fuck it," Hannah said. "There's no one around. Let's go au naturel."

The two girls unclasped their bras then pulled their panties off and scampered into the waterfall, laughing as the water splashed against their bare chest and asses.

"What are you guys waiting for?" Hannah said, looking at the rest of us hesitating on the bank of the waterfall. "It's warm, clean, and refreshing. Strip off your clothes and join us!"

The four of us glanced at one another for a few seconds, then we quickly disrobed and joined Hannah and Lilly in the waterfall. At first it was a bit of a shock feeling the cool water on my hot skin, but it didn't take long to get used to it. After a few minutes, it felt just like a warm shower.

I'd barely had a chance to glimpse at the naked bodies of the other girls before they scrambled into the waterfall, but with the running water tumbling over us, it was a feast to take in. We were all in good shape from regular yoga and gym classes, but there was something about Emma's figure that I couldn't take my eyes off. She had a more slender, youthful figure, and I stole glances at her pointed nipples on her perky breasts as the water cascading over her tight chest and abdomen. Her bare pussy shined in the sunlight as the liquid fingers teased and danced over her glistening mound.

"What'd I tell you?" Hannah said, blinking at me as the water crashed over her head. "Isn't it glorious? Warm, refreshing, and *unspoiled*."

Lilly tipped her head as she opened her mouth wide under the falling water.

"Feel free to rehydrate," she gurgled. "This is the cleanest water you'll find just about anywhere on earth. Lop it up!"

We all tilted our heads back and giggled and spat at one another as we stretched our arms out, feeling the warm current passing over us. After a few minutes, Lilly began tiptoeing over the steep rocks lining the waterfall toward the other side of the cataract.

"Come on, you guys," she said. "There's something else I want to show you. Just be careful as you step on these slippery rocks. I don't want anybody falling down the waterfall."

"Um, *yeah*," I said, glancing down the steep embankment to the bottom of the waterfall thirty feet below.

We followed Lilly through the falling water, grasping onto the sides of exposed outcroppings to make sure we had a firm handhold and stepping carefully onto the rocks to be sure we had a solid footing. When we all got to the other side, she giggled and ran off into the bush. We had no idea where she was going, but after about twenty feet through the thick brush, we stopped at the top of a sheer cliff overlooking a lake thirty feet below.

We stood there for a moment trying not to gape at each other's wet naked bodies, then peered at Lilly warily.

"What do you say?" she said. "Are you guys game?"

"What?!" Madison exclaimed. "You mean *jump*? Off *this*? Down *there*?"

"Are you *crazy*?" Bonnie said. "We'll *kill* ourselves!"

"It's only thirty feet or so," Lilly said. "I've done it plenty of times. It doesn't even hurt. Just be sure to put your hands over your peachka and keep your legs together so you don't get too much of a slap between your legs. Last one in is a pussy!"

Lilly screeched as she jumped off the cliff while we peered over the ledge and watched her splash into the still water below. Five seconds later, she emerged from under the surface and screamed with delight as she motioned for us to follow.

We all looked at one another with wide eyes, then Hannah, Bonnie, and Madison followed soon after. I glanced at Emma with a mix of trepidation and lust. Part of my hesitation was not wanting to be the last one following the girls into the pool below, but the other part of me just wanted to stay on top and take in Emma's sweet nubile body as long as I could. She kept her body shyly turned away from me so I couldn't see her bare mound while she quivered holding her arms tightly across her chest. The other girls were taunting us from below and I knew that sooner or later one of us would have to go.

"Are you up for this?" I said, watching her quaking in fear.

"I dunno," Emma said. "It's a long way down."

"How about if we hold hands and do it together?" I said.

Emma looked at me uncertainly for a moment, then nodded and edged closer to me. Then she held out her hand and I clasped it gently. I could feel her hand shaking, and I squeezed it to build her confidence.

"On the count of three, okay?" I said.

Emma nodded as I began the count.

"One...two...*three*!" I yelled as Emma and I leaped off the cliff together into the bracing water below.

That wasn't the only leap that Emma and I would take over the next few days.

2

NIGHT WHISPERS

We swam for a few minutes in the warm water of the lake below the waterfall, then retrieved our gear and completed our portage down to the shore. The experience of paddling the canoes across the quiet lake was sublime. There was virtually no noise other than the occasional cry of a bird and the soft sloshing sound of our paddles dipping in and out of the water. Little black bugs skittered over the surface as the bows of our canoes sliced through the shimmering liquid. Every now and then I'd hear a droplet sound near our boat followed by little concentric ripples in the water.

"What's that sound?" I asked Lilly, who'd taken up the stern position in my canoe. "It sounds like someone throwing pebbles in the water."

"It's fish feasting on all those water skeeters," she said. "They're a pretty tempting snack just sitting there on the surface."

"What *kind* of fish?" Hannah asked, peering over the gunwale into the dark water from her squatted position in the middle of our canoe. "Should we be worried about us being fish food for some kind of monster dwelling under the surface? It's pretty dark down there. I can barely see two feet below the surface."

Lilly chuckled as she dragged her paddle in the water to steer our canoe gently to the starboard side.

"The water's actually remarkably clear when you're underneath it. But you needn't worry about any Jaws-like predator under the surface. It's mostly filled with Walleye, Pike, Bass, and Yellow Perch. Though some of the Muskies do grow to five or six feet in length, they only have teeth big enough to eat smaller fish."

Hannah peered over to the other canoe knifing through the water a few feet away.

"What about *Emma*?" she said, smiling at the cute girl next to us. "By those standards, I'd say she qualifies as 'smaller fish'. You better watch out you don't get gobbled up by one of those things, Emma!"

Emma turned her head in Hannah's direction and peered over her sunglasses, then continued quietly paddling the front of her canoe. I watched her toned arms rippling and her little breasts shaking on her chest as her ass wiggled on her seat from the paddling motion.

"Where's a good place to set up camp?" I asked Lilly.

She looked around the lake and saw a small rocky outcropping about half a mile to our northeast.

"There's an island over that way," she said pointing to the peninsula. "We should have it all to ourselves, and if I remember correctly, there's a quiet little bay behind it that should make for perfect bass fishing. We can all give it a try later and see if we can catch something fresh for dinner."

"When you say all to *ourselves*, do you mean no bears?" I asked.

Lilly chuckled at my first-time camping trepidation.

"I meant in terms of other campers. We probably won't run into anybody else this far from civilization, but I did notice another car in the parking lot at our trailhead. As for bears, they're pretty good swimmers, but as long as we keep our food locked up and sealed, they should leave us alone."

"I'm not sure I'm comfortable with the *should* part of that statement," I said.

When we got to the island, we found a small beach and pulled our canoes ashore. We unpacked the boats and located a flat mossy section in the center of the island to pitch our three tents. There were six girls, with each tent comfortably accommodating two air mattresses and two sleeping bags. We contemplated drawing straws to see who would sleep with whom, then we all just giggled and threw our gear in whichever tent was closest. Hannah joined me, Maddie and Lilly took the next, and Emma and Bonnie took the last. I peered over at Emma's tent as she got down on her knees and wiggled her ass through the front canopy, suddenly wishing I'd joined her.

After we set up camp, we set out in pairs to collect kindling and driftwood for a fire, then we had a refreshing swim in our bikinis to cool off. I was surprised how hot it got by mid-afternoon, and the water, though still warm, provided a handy respite from the heat. Soon after, Lilly collected the fishing rods and tackle, and we all walked over to the far end of the island overlooking a small bay filled with water lilies.

"Now I see why you like to come here," Hannah chuckled, scanning the idyllic scene. "It's filled with your favorite type of flowers."

"Yeah, well those lilies also provide perfect cover for bass and perch. We've got our own little seafood restaurant hiding under those pretty flowers."

She reached down onto the ground and picked up a fishing rod.

"Who knows how to use these things?"

We all just looked at her dumbfounded.

"No worries," she said. "Let me show you how it's done."

She connected the loose pieces of the shaft then attached a red and white striped metal lure to the end of the fishing line. Then she stepped about ten feet back from our group and looked out over the shore.

"Okay," she said. "The most important thing is that you don't snare yourself or anyone else as you're casting your line into the water. Which is why you'll need to separate yourself from your next nearest fisherwoman by at least ten to fifteen feet."

"Fisherwoman?" I teased. "Is that what your grandpappy used to call you?"

"Not exactly. But hey, there's no guys out here, so I'm improvising. Fisherperson, fisherman, angler, whatever. Now listen up. After I get your rods and lures assembled, you hold the rod like this."

Lilly held the rod out firmly in front of her, gripping the cork handle.

"Like you're giving it a firm handshake, with your middle and forefingers threaded under the handle of the reel."

"Or like you're giving it a firm hand job," Hannah snickered.

"Now..." Lilly continued, rolling her eyes. "Hold the rod out beside you and make sure you've got about two feet of line hanging down from the tip of the rod, like this."

"Like a horny cock dripper..." Hannah said, continuing the metaphor.

"Behave, Hannah," Lilly admonished her friend, "or I'm gonna slap your ass. Now, press and hold this little release button on your reel, then turn your body sideways, holding the rod out in front of you. Then swing your arm quickly out in the direction you want your lure to land and release the button just before you get to the end, like this."

Lilly deftly swung the rod with her wrist and we watched her lure sail about forty feet over the water and plop just short of a bunch of water lilies.

"I'm attaching bobbers to the ends of your lines so you shouldn't have to worry about your line getting caught on rocks underwater."

"*Bobbers? Rods? Swinging?*" Hannah joked. "You gotta admit it sounds a bit like—"

"Put your dick in your pants, Hannah," Lilly said. "Try to concentrate, will you, so we all don't starve out here?

"When you cast your lure," she continued, "try not to get too close to the flowers or your line will get caught up there too. You may need to practice a few times to get the hang of it, but after a few swings, you should be casting like a champ. After your lure lands in the water, start turning the crank on the reel counterclockwise slowly so your lure will swim through the water looking like a real fish."

"What if we *catch* something?" Bonnie asked.

"You'll feel a tug on your line and some sudden tension in your reel. Just steady your rod and crank the fish in slowly toward shore. Give me a shout if you need any help. Once your fish gets close to shore, I'll use my net to land him. Then I'll tie him up to this little stringer to keep him fresh underwater until we eat."

"Until you chop off his head and gut and cook him, you mean," Hannah joked.

Emma hunched her shoulders and winced.

"Poor little fishes," she said. "They'll just be going about minding their own business when suddenly a hook tears into their flesh. Then we'll yank them by their mouth out of their element and tie them up while they wait to be guillotined. How barbaric!"

"Hey, it's a fish-eat-fish world out there, Emms," Lilly chuckled. "We just happen to be the biggest fish at the top of the food chain. If I remember correctly, we don't have any vegetarians among us, do we?"

Lilly paused for a moment to make sure everybody was on board.

"Right, let's get started then. If anybody wants to sit this one out and just watch the rest of us, that's cool. If we're feeling generous, we might share some of our catch with you later."

Lilly proceeded to assemble each of our rods, then we separated along the bank and awkwardly practiced casting into the bay. It didn't take me too long to get the hang of it, and after five or six casts I was able to fling my lure almost as far as Lilly with similar accuracy. I glanced over at Emma standing fifteen feet to my right and noticed her huffing and cursing as her lure jerked and plopped into the water only a few feet in front of her.

I stepped behind her and reached around, grasping her rod with my two hands.

"Hey, Emma," I said. "Let me see if I can help you. The key is in timing the button release at the right moment."

I positioned Emma's thumb over the button on the reel, then placed my thumb over hers. Then I pulled the rod gently behind us a few feet and swung her arms forward in a sudden jerk.

"*Release!*" I yelled as we watched her lure go sailing twenty feet into the bay.

"Yayyyy!" Emma squealed with delight.

Then she turned around and kissed me on the cheek.

"Thanks, Jade. You're an awesome fisherwoman. Don't go too far away. I still might need you to show me how to wiggle my hips properly to make this work."

I looked into Emma's eyes and smiled as I felt my cheeks warm with a gentle flush.

"You got it, girl," I said. "I'll keep one eye on you from my perch right over there."

Truth was, I kept more than one eye on her wiggling ass in her tight bikini as she continued casting her rod. After about ten minutes of quiet casting into the still waters of the bay, Emma suddenly began hyperventilating.

"I think I've got something!" she squealed, as we watched the tip of her rod twitch and bend in frenetic tugs.

"Okay, Emm," Lilly said, rushing over. "Just hold your rod steady and slowly crank the handle of your reel away from you. There's no rush—let him tucker himself out for a bit before you try to outmuscle him."

She looked at the deep bend in Lilly's rod and nodded.

"It looks like a big one, maybe a five-pounder. That might be enough to feed all of us tonight. Be cool, girl—take your time. Just remember, you're stronger than he is."

We all cheered Emma on as she struggled to control her fluttering rod and awkwardly reel in the fish. When it got close to shore, it jumped two feet out of the water and waved twice rapidly in the air before diving back under the surface.

Lilly stepped down onto the bank with a fishnet and

stepped into the water as the fish neared shore, then swung the net underwater and lifted it up for us to see. As the bass flapped wildly in the tangled rope, Lilly calmly reached down and removed the hook from its mouth. Then she threaded her fingers under its gills and held the fish up for everybody to see.

"Woo-hoo!" Emma yelped, proud that she'd caught the first fish of the day.

"Good job, Emm," Hannah said, and we all clapped and smiled to acknowledge her accomplishment.

Lilly attached Emma's catch to the stringer chain underwater, then the group fished for another thirty minutes until we'd caught three more bass.

"That should do it if you guys want to take a breather," Lilly said, placing the stringer of fish in a metal pail filled with water. "Time to cook these fellas up and see what real Canadian food tastes like."

The sun was beginning to lower on the horizon, and after taking another short swim to cool off, we all got dressed in cargo pants and polar fleeces to protect ourselves against the mosquitos and evening chill. I watched Lilly deftly cut off the head of each fish then expertly fillet the flesh to remove it from the thin skeleton underneath.

"Looks like you've done this before," I said, marveling at her skill.

"A few hundred times maybe," she said.

I stood mesmerized as she sliced the fish under its belly and removed its entrails, then carefully pulled the flanks away from the spiny skeleton inside.

"Kind of messy, huh?"

"Yeah, it's a bit gross at first, but you get used to it pretty quick. My mouth is already watering thinking about the taste."

While Lilly filleted the fish, the other girls collected

some small logs and rocks from around the shore and placed them in concentric circles in the middle of our campsite to build a fire pit. Then they placed some twigs and driftwood inside the rocky pit and started a small fire. After it quieted down a bit, Lilly placed a steel grate and a cast iron pan over the hole and slapped a few slivers of butter in the pan along with the fillets. Before long, the aroma of fresh pan-seared fish wafted into the air.

"That smells exquisite, Lilly," Hannah said, suddenly emerging from her tent. "Do you need us to help prepare any sides?"

Lilly shook her head.

"For our first night together, I just want you to savor this, straight-up. All we need to finish it off is some lemon slices cut up and some paper plates and forks."

When the fish was done, we all sat around the campfire on the wooden logs while Lilly served us our plates.

"*Oh my God,* Lilly," Bonnie said, placing the first morsel in her mouth, closing her eyes and tilting her head back. "This is to *die* for! Now I don't feel nearly as bad about yanking those little critters out of their cozy lily garden."

"What about *you*, Emma?" Lilly said, glancing in her direction. "Are you comfortable with eating your catch?"

"Um, *yeah*," Emma said, as she gobbled the fish down.

"Mmmm," Hannah chimed in. "What *is* it exactly that makes this so good? This tastes even better than at the top-rated seafood restaurant in the city."

"Who knows?" Emma said, shaking her head. "It could just be because we're eating it truly fresh-caught. Maybe it's the lemon and butter seasoning."

"Or maybe it's just that pristine freshwater Canadian goodness coming through," I joked.

After we finished eating, Lilly placed the entrails and

fish heads back in the water, then we washed our cutlery and bagged up our plates and hung our trash from a rope over a high tree branch to keep the bears away. As dusk set in, we built our fire back up and huddled around the pit in a circle.

"What now?" Hannah said. "What do six girls do for fun after dark on a lonely island in the middle of nowhere? Tell spooky stories?"

"*Stories* could be fun," Maddie said. "But they don't have to be spooky. I'm already creeped out enough about the idea of sleeping in that flimsy tent with so many bears within swimming distance. How about some *fun* stories?"

"I know!" Bonnie said. "Let play *Truth or Dare*. That outta get our juices going. Who wants to go first?"

"Truth, or *dare*?" Hannah asked.

"Truth," Bonnie said. "Tell us something daring about yourself that none of us know."

"Hmmm," Hannah said, looking up trying to think of some sordid detail from her past that she was willing to share. "Well—I once spent a night in jail."

"No way!" Emma said, her eyes widening in disbelief.

"*Way*," Hannah said. "Though granted it was only for a couple of hours. I was sixteen and got caught for shoplifting. I think the sheriff in my small town wanted to make an example of me to scare the shit out of me."

"Did it work?" Lilly asked.

"I wasn't really scared, because I was all alone in my cell and I kind of knew what they were trying to do. I was more scared about what my father was going to do to me when he bailed me out."

"And?" I said.

"Grounded for three months. Which is like three *years*

when you're sixteen. So yeah, I guess it worked insofar as discouraging me from doing something like that again."

"What did you steal?" Bonnie asked.

"A vibrator from the local sex shop. I was too embarrassed to actually buy it, so I tried to sneak it out under my coat instead."

"That'll teach you to play with naughty things before your time," Lilly winked at Hannah.

"What about *you*, Lil?" Hannah said. "What naughty things have you done that we don't know about?"

"*Welll*," Lilly said, stretching out the word for dramatic effect. "I engaged in some technically illegal sex not too long ago...."

"Mmmm, *yummy*," Hannah said. "Do tell. There's not many things that are illegal anymore in that area."

"It was an underage boy. *Sixteen* to be exact. The captain of my son's football team. We were at the boy's parents' house celebrating their championship and he and I were alone having a chat, and one thing led to another. We slipped into the ravine behind his yard and had a quickie."

"A *quickie*?" Hannah teased. "That hardly sounds like fun. Was he nicely hung at least?"

"He definitely came equipped with a decent package. But you know boys at that age. They can't last very long—"

"What exactly did you two do?" I probed for more details.

"I just gave him a quick blowjob. I was too terrified we'd be found out. But it was fun and definitely satisfying."

"For at least *one* of you!" Madison said.

"I suppose," Lilly said. "How about you, Maddie? What kinky things have you gotten into that we don't know about?"

Maddie paused for a moment trying to conjure up a sufficiently juicy story.

"Well, my husband and I just had anal sex for the first time last week—"

"Which *one*?" Hannah said. "You or *him*?"

"*Hannah!*" Bonnie scolded, shooting Hannah a disapproving look. "That's prying a little too deep. Let Maddie tell the story."

"What?" Hannah said. "I'm just saying, she could have used a strap-on, or something. Some guys are into that sort of thing—"

"It was *me*, if you must know," Maddie said. "I mean *receiving*, that is."

"What's that like?" Emma said, scrunching up her nose in disgust. "I mean, doesn't it hurt?"

"Oooh," Hannah teased. "I guess we know at least *one* of us has never tried this. Poor little Emma, leading such a sheltered life..."

Emma lowered her head and frowned as she peered into the fire. I wanted to walk over to her log and put my arms around her. It was cruel of Hannah to put her on the spot like that and make her feel small.

"Well it didn't hurt exactly," Maddie continued. "But I wouldn't say I enjoyed it as much as the usual way. My husband certainly did though, judging by his moans of delight."

Everybody paused for a moment as the girls looked at me and Emma to see who would go next. Hannah glanced over at Emma still sulking on her log and finally broke the silence.

"What about you, Jade? What kind of fun adventures have you been up to lately? I mean besides sleeping in and working on your graphic design projects?"

I looked at Hannah with a sly smile. If she *only* knew. I probably had accumulated enough kinky stories just in the last couple of months to outdo everybody around the campfire. But I still wasn't ready to share my most personal secret.

"Well, I recently had a little remote affair with one of my neighbors..." I started.

"*Remote*?" Hannah said. "As in not face-to-face? Was it telephone sex or webcam sex?"

"Neither. We just watched each other through our windows at night. It was actually pretty hot."

"Oh? Is this someone you've had your eye on for a while? Is he hot? What did you guys do?"

"Yes, I've had my eye on him for a while now," I lied, not wanting to tell the girls that it was actually Abby, the college girl next door. "We've been watching each other around our adjoining pools for some time. But he's married, so I never felt comfortable making the first move."

"So, what did he do? Flash you from his private study while his wife was doing the dishes?"

"I think his wife was away for a few days. It was late at night, and I caught him coming out of the shower with his bedroom light on. I guess he caught me watching him and one thing led to another..."

"So you both rubbed one out watching each other?"

"Yeah. But it was just a one-time thing. His wife came home the next day and I didn't want to take any more chances at getting caught."

"Well that definitely qualifies as semi-hot," Lilly said.

Everybody turned to Emma, who glanced nervously out of the corner of her eyes at the rest of the group.

"That just leaves you, Em," Lilly said. "What sordid details have you been holding back about yourself?"

Emma paused for a long moment as she glanced at her friends around the campfire.

"Well, I once did it with a...*girl*. You know, at college."

My panties instantly moistened as I squirmed uncomfortably on my log.

"It was with my roommate. We were both pretty drunk after a party, so I'm not even sure it qualifies—"

"Oh, I think it *definitely* qualifies," Hannah said. "You've got to give us at least a few details. What did you two do exactly?"

"You know, the usual stuff. There's only so many things two girls can do together, right?"

"*Boo!*" Hannah jeered. "Not good enough. You've got to give us at least one detail."

"Well," Emma hesitated. "It started with us both lamenting how neither of us had hooked up in a long time. One thing led to another, and we ended up making out on my bed."

The more I listened to Emma, the more I could feel a large wet spot spreading in my cargo pants between my legs. I shimmied toward a knot on my log and quietly rubbed my clit against the stump in the dark as Emma told her story.

"*Making out*?" Hannah said. "What do you mean? Kissed, fondled, sucked, scissored—we want details!"

I could see Emma shifting nervously on her log, beginning to feel uncomfortable about sharing any more details.

"You know," I interrupted. This whole time we've been telling truths and we haven't even had a single dare. I've got a dare for everybody. I dare you all to strip off your clothes and go skinny dipping in the lake with the big old muskies and snapping turtles!"

"If we don't get eaten alive by the *mosquitoes* first!" Bonnie protested.

"Not if we get in the water fast enough," I said, stripping off my clothes. "Last one in a rotten egg!" I scampered over the pine needles of our campsite and ran into the water at our little beach.

"Come on in, you scaredy-cats!" I taunted from the water. "The water's warmer than the air. It's like taking a bath."

The rest of the girls quickly disrobed and scurried into the water, where we splashed and spit water at each other's faces and playfully dove under the surface groping each other. After about ten minutes, we all scampered out of the water and toweled dry, then rushed into our tents and zipped up the flaps to keep the mosquitoes out.

I scolded Hannah for putting Emma on the spot earlier, then we talked a little bit about work before falling asleep early from all the sun and fresh air. But about thirty minutes later, I woke to the sound of rustling not far from our tent. Thinking it might be a bear foraging through our camp, I was about to wake Hannah when I heard the unmistakable sound of a woman moaning. I lay perfectly still and held my breath straining to listen.

The sound was coming from the direction of Bonnie and Emma's tent. I lifted the privacy flap up over the mosquito net window on my side of the tent and peered into the darkness. They'd left a small flashlight on inside their tent, and I could see the shadows of two figures lying next to one another, rubbing their bodies together.

They're making out! I thought.

Suddenly, I wished I'd tried harder to pair up with Emma in her tent. I was envious of Bonnie having her all to herself. Obviously, Emma's story had gotten more than just *me* worked up, and after they'd returned to their tent stark naked, one thing had led to another.

Fuck! I whispered out loud, thrusting my hand under my sleeping bag, beginning to circle my clit.

As I strained to catch whatever I could pick up from the tent next door, I began to hear gasps and moans radiating into the still night. I couldn't make out if it was Emma's or Bonnie's voice, or both of them. But it didn't matter. I was insanely turned on just listening to them, trying to imagine what the two of them were doing.

I squinted through the mosquito netting trying to discern their movement, but I just saw a jumbled clump of shadows shifting in the soft backlight. Suddenly, one of the figures rolled on top of the other, and I saw the unmistakable shape of a naked ass raising and lowering onto the person beneath.

Oh my God. Now they're humping each other!

I wanted to dash out of my tent and join the girls in their fun and feel Emma's sweet pussy between my own legs. *Oh —how much pleasure I could give her,* I thought. I sped up the movement of my fingers over my clit, trying to control my breathing and movement so as not to wake Hannah.

Suddenly, the figure on top raised up to a kneeling position and the girl on the bottom pulled her legs up into a bent knee position. Then the girl on top squatted over her and lowered herself onto her partner below. When the girl on top began shimmying her hips, I saw her full breasts swaying in the backlight and realized for the first time that Emma was on the bottom.

Emma doesn't have tits that full and round, I thought. *Bonnie's full-on fucking her!*

I could hear the women's breathing becoming louder and more ragged, building toward a climax. I jammed two fingers into my cunt and began thrusting as hard as I dared without waking Hannah from the squeaking of my air mattress shifting on the soft ground below us.

Suddenly, the moans escalated in urgency, as Emma thrashed her head from side to side in the throes of pleasure.

"Yes, Bonnie!" I heard her whisper. "Fuck me harder. I'm going to come!"

My pussy suddenly clamped down on my fingers as my orgasm washed over me, and I bit my lip trying to stifle my moans.

"I'm coming, Bonnie!" Emma whispered. "Come with me! Fuuuck—I'm coming!"

Bonnie sped up the humping motion of her hips against Emma, then she suddenly stopped as I saw her chest and torso jerking spastically in the soft backlight.

"Uhnnn," she grunted, as she came inside Emma's sweet tight pussy. "Fuck, yes," she said. "I'm coming, baby!"

I twitched and spasmed inside my sleeping bag as I came along with the two girls, trying desperately not to awaken Hannah sleeping mere inches beside me. When Bonnie finally collapsed on top of Emma and their light switched off, I rubbed out two more orgasms before falling blissfully asleep with the warm stickiness between my legs.

3

BEST FRIENDS

I woke to the cry of a loon echoing over the still lake. Hannah was still sleeping, so I put on some warm clothes and quietly unzipped the front of our tent. Lilly and Madison were huddled around the fire pit with some mugs in their hands and I joined them.

"Morning, Jade," Lilly said. "Did you sleep well?"

"Like a baby. It must be all this fresh air and clean living. Hannah and I fell fast asleep shortly after our swim last night."

"No bear nightmares or intrusions?" Lilly chuckled.

"No, thank God," I said, wondering if Lilly and Maddie had heard the noise from Bonnie and Emma's tent. "Though I *did* hear some other rustling around the camp..."

"Oh?" Lilly said. "It might have been raccoons trying to steal our leftovers."

She looked up at the high tree branch where our garbage bag from last night still dangled twenty feet off the ground.

"Looks like they weren't able to solve our little challenge."

She handed me a steaming mug filled with dark fluid.

"Would you like some hot chocolate? Sorry we don't have fresh coffee, but we couldn't exactly fit a coffee maker in our backpacks."

I nodded at Lilly and took the mug between my two hands to warm my fingers.

"We're really roughing it, eh?" I said.

"Good one!" Lilly smiled at me. "You see—you're already starting to sound like a real Canadian."

I peered out across the quiet lake and marveled at the serene beauty of the landscape. The water was smooth as glass, and the sunrise reflected over the surface in a dimpled crimson glow. Tall evergreen trees rose from the rocky shore surrounding the lake, and there was no sign of movement other than a pair of low-flying geese skimming low over the water.

"It's gorgeous out here. You were right, Lilly. It's just as magnificent as you said it would be."

I took a sip of my hot chocolate, then peered up at her.

"So, what's on the agenda today? More skinny dipping and fish-wrangling?"

Lilly chuckled.

"We'll wait 'til the rest of the girls get up. But I was thinking maybe another canoe ride and some more exploring. There's so much natural beauty to explore up here. We can try trolling for fish in the deep water. Maybe we'll catch a pike or a muskie. That'd be enough to feed us for a whole week!"

I heard the sound of a zipper opening as Hannah stepped out of our tent groggily.

"Morning, sleepy-head!" I called out. "Who's the lazy morning person *now*?"

"Ha!" Hannah said, taking a seat beside me on the log.

"We're supposed to be chilling up here, remember? I haven't slept this well in a long time."

"So you didn't hear our little visitor last night?" I asked, probing to see if she'd been woken up by Bonnie and Emma's little play date.

"We had a *visitor*?"

"I just heard a bit of rustling around the camp." I glanced up toward our hanging trash bag. "Lilly thinks it might have been a raccoon trying to reach our little waste receptacle."

"Speaking of," Hannah said. "I think I need to do a little disposal of my own. What's the protocol up here?"

Lilly reached behind her log and threw Hannah a roll of toilet paper.

"Do as the bears do," she said. "There's a small spade over by the tree. If you can dig a shallow hole and bury it when you're done, it'll help keep the place clean for other campers."

"Man—" Hannah huffed, "we really *are* roughing it, aren't we?"

Shortly after Hannah trudged off into the brush behind us, Emma and Bonnie emerged from their tent. I was glad that no one other than me had apparently heard them frolicking last night, as they approached our group tentatively. I poured some hot water from the steaming pot on the fire into two empty mugs, then emptied two packets of hot chocolate mix into the water and stirred it with a small stick.

"Hey, you two," I said, handing them each a mug. "Welcome to the party. Did you sleep well?"

Emma took a seat on the log beside me and glanced at Bonnie out the corner of her eye.

"Yes," she said. "It was very...*relaxing*. Those air mattresses are surprisingly comfortable. How about you guys?"

I didn't think it would be proper to mention the

suspected 'raccoon' invasion that disrupted the camp last night.

"Slept like a baby," I said.

I glanced at Emma's bare legs in her cargo shorts and noticed a pink glow.

"I think maybe you got a little too much sun yesterday, Emma."

I reached into my fanny pack and pulled out some sunscreen.

"You might want to put a little protection on. Lilly's suggesting we go for another canoe excursion today. You'll be fully exposed out there on the water."

Emma accepted the bottle and began spreading the lotion across the inside and top of her thighs. I tried not to stare, but her skin blushed and blanched as she pressed her fingers into her soft flesh.

"Actually, you might want to wear your cargo pants to cover up," Lilly said. "I can tell you from experience how easy it is to get a nasty sunburn spending the whole day out on the water."

Hannah suddenly interrupted us as she traipsed out of the brush.

"That was fun." She held the toilet paper roll up for everybody to see. "Anybody else need to take a go?"

We all shook our heads and Hannah placed the shovel and roll behind the log next to Bonnie as she sat down beside her.

"So what's the plan for today? More sexy stories and skinny dipping? What else can six girls do in the middle of nowhere?"

Emma and Bonnie shifted uncomfortably on their logs, and the group paused for a moment in awkward silence.

"Lilly suggested a little canoe excursion," I said. "We could explore the surrounding countryside a bit more."

Hannah peered around the lake as she listened to the sound of frogs chirping from the lily pond.

"Doesn't look like there's much more to discover out here than pine cones and bullfrogs."

"We can try to track down one of those *bears* if you're looking for a bit more excitement," Lilly said. "Or maybe some rattlesnakes. There's a lot more interesting wildlife out here than you might imagine. Don't be such a party-pooper, Hannah."

"Rattlesnakes?" Emma said, her eyes suddenly widening. "You didn't mention *those* before heading out."

"I didn't want to scare you guys away. I figured that might tip the balance. But don't worry. They'll give you plenty of warning if you get too close. You've got a better chance of getting hit by a car in the city than being bitten by a snake out here."

She reached behind her log and opened a cooler, then held out a couple of eggs and a pack of bacon.

"But first, who's up for a real woodsman's breakfast? Cooked up real authentic-like on the griddle?"

"Hell, yes!" Hannah exclaimed. "I could eat a moose right now."

After a hearty breakfast of scrambled eggs and pan-fried Canadian bacon, we set out in our two canoes to explore the lake. There were lots of bays and gullies in the meandering shoreline, and I marveled at the quiet and serene beauty of the craggy landscape. Some of the girls tried trolling for fish behind our canoes, but no one caught anything and by midday, our stomachs were grumbling again. Lilly suggested we put in on a larger island to forage for firewood since we'd already collected most of the loose driftwood on our own little islet.

We beached our canoes on the new island and decided to pair up to go exploring. The island was quite large with lots of tall pine, spruce, and fir trees providing ample shade from the hot overhead sun. But the trek was slow-going, with many fallen trees and lichen-covered rocks to sidestep. The girls had decided to pair up again based on their previous tent assignments, and I was beginning to despair of ever finding any alone time with Emma.

We spread out in different directions over the large island. After thirty minutes or so of exploring with Hannah, I caught a glimpse of two bodies reflecting in a shaded glade. I stopped and peered in their direction and realized it was Bonnie and Emma. They were topless and making out behind a large tree! Hannah looked back at me wondering what was holding me up, and I told her I had to stop to take care of some business and that I'd catch up with her.

As she moved further ahead, I slowly crept closer to Bonnie and Emma's position. It was hard to stay quiet with all the loose twigs and rocks on the ground, but I managed to get within about thirty feet of them without being detected. When I got close to their alcove, I ducked behind a large stump and saw that Emma had removed all of her clothing and was sitting on a fallen tree with her legs spread apart. Bonnie knelt between her legs bobbing her head up and down.

Fuck! I thought. *She's licking her pussy! Right in the middle of the forest!*

I quickly dropped my pants and began rubbing my cunt furiously. I had to fight hard to control my breathing and movement so as not to be detected as I gritted my teeth trying to contain my pleasure. Emma arched her back and placed her hands beside Bonnie's ears then pulled her head into her snatch. I could hear her grunting and moaning, and it took every ounce of my energy to remain silent.

As I hunched down behind my tree stump trying to keep my head hidden, suddenly a twig broke underfoot and I ducked under the stump to hide from the girls. I could hear them stop for a moment as they looked around to ensure they were alone, then Emma's moaning resumed. When I peered back over the log, my eyes met with Emma's and we froze for a moment realizing we'd seen each other. But she didn't ask Bonnie to stop and instead pulled her head harder into her pussy as she stared at me through glistening eyes. I kept my head down just enough to stay hidden if Bonnie turned around, while I watched Emma get eaten out.

Emma began rocking her hips and as she pulled Bonnie into her, I could tell that she was close. I raised up just enough for Emma to see my face while I squeezed my breast with one hand and jilled myself with the other. Emma must have noticed my movement and known what I was doing, and the sight of seeing each other getting turned on watching the other, ramped up our arousal even more.

Emma stared straight at me as she began panting louder, then she nodded as if signaling that she was ready. That was all I needed and I gushed all over my fallen pants as I watched Emma's head bob and jerk in quiet climax. After a minute or so, Bonnie and Emma began to get dressed and I ducked under my tree stump to collect myself. For now, at least, this private moment of pleasure would remain between Emma and me.

When I caught up with Hannah, she looked at the wet dribbles on the front of my pants and shook her head.

"Girl, you've got to learn how to shit in the woods properly. The trick is to find a rock or tree stump to support yourself. If you're going to squat down, the least you can do is take your pants off first."

"Yeah," I said. "A tree stump sounds like a good idea. Next time."

"I can't take you anywhere, Jade. We're going to have to get you hooked up right soon before you devolve into a blubbering baby."

I just nodded quietly as I followed Hannah along the trail through the forest.

After we collected some firewood, we all reconvened at the beach where we'd set in and built another fire pit. Then we sharpened some sticks and cooked some wieners Lilly had packed in the cooler. Neither Emma nor I talked about what we'd seen, but I noticed her looking in my direction frequently with a knowing smile.

After lunch, we set out again in the canoes and found another tall cliff to jump off, then we cavorted in the water and lay in the sun to dry off. Madison caught a big pike trolling behind her canoe, and when we returned to our little island later in the day, Lilly cooked it up in the skillet and we roasted marshmallows telling more fun stories. I kept glancing at Emma, wondering if we were ever going to have a chance to be alone, but around midnight all of us retired to our regular tents.

After we slipped into our respective sleeping bags, Hannah turned to me and smiled.

"Are you enjoying our camping experience so far?" she asked.

"Yes," I said. "This is nice for a change. It's good to get away. You were right, Han. I really needed this. Thanks for inviting me."

Hannah paused for a long moment.

"Did you have fun on the island today?" she said.

"Um, yes. I enjoyed the hike and the hot dog roast—you know, just communing with the girls..."

"I saw you watching Emma and Bonnie."

"What?" I said, feeling a flush roll over my cheeks. "You mean when I held back to take care of some business?"

"That wasn't the only business I saw you taking care of. It's okay, you know. You don't have to hide it from me. We're supposed to be best friends. If you like girls that way, it doesn't change anything between us."

I hesitated, unsure how best to respond, then exhaled deeply, realizing I didn't need to hide my attraction to women any longer.

"It was just...*hot*, you know? Watching them go at it like wild animals in the wilderness. I couldn't stop looking..."

"I know. Neither could I. You weren't the only one enjoying the show."

I turned my head toward Hannah and looked at her surprised.

"You too? Are you—"

"I still prefer men. But you have to admit, Emma is pretty hot. I've had my eye on her for a while too. I heard you last night listening to them."

I gasped and sat up on top of my sleeping bag.

"You were sure *faking* it pretty well! Pretending to be asleep the whole time."

"How could I? With you moving your hand between

your legs so rapidly under the covers and your air mattress squeaking away."

"Why didn't you say something?"

"I didn't want to interrupt your fun. Besides, I was getting just as turned on as you. I rubbed a couple of quiet ones out listening to you and the other girls. Besides, we're friends. I didn't know if you'd wanted to..."

I looked into Hannah's eyes, suddenly realizing how sexy she was. I'd always admired her beauty, but had never thought of it beyond that. But now that I saw her sitting with the soft glow of the moonlight from our open tent window reflecting off her bare breasts, she looked like much more than just a close friend to me.

I leaned over to her side of the tent and kissed her softly on her lips. She shifted her hips closer to mine and we began kissing more passionately, intertwining our tongues in each other's mouths. When she pressed her tits against mine, we both began moaning.

"Damn, girl," she said, pulling away from me for a moment. "Can you believe we've waited all these years to do this?"

Then she crawled out of her sleeping bag and began to unzip the side of my bedroll. She flipped the cover over and straddled my naked body. Then she began kissing my neck and working her way down my body. When she got to my breasts, she sucked on my teats gently, swirling her tongue around my nipples as I held her cheeks gently between my two hands. I tried to pull her up to kiss her again, but she pushed me down on my air mattress and continued nibbling her way toward my pussy. When she got to my belly button she paused, blowing kisses into my little hole, then gently kissed her way to the bony edges of my pelvis.

"For somebody who doesn't like girls," I said, panting in

anticipation, "you sure know your way around a female body."

"Who said I didn't like girls?" she said, glancing up at me.

"But you said you prefer—"

"Just shut up, will you?" she said, stretching her hand up to my chin and placing it gently over my mouth. "Lie back and enjoy this. I've been wanting to do this for quite a while."

Hannah extended her tongue and traced a line down the ridge of my hipbone toward my steaming pussy. I lifted my hips, inviting her to go lower, but she paused on top of my mound and rubbed her cheeks softly against my pubis.

"You're so soft," she purred. "Somebody's had some work done recently."

Then she lowered her head between my legs and placed her open mouth directly over my hard clit and began sucking it into her mouth. I moaned and gyrated my hips in pleasure as I ran my fingers through her soft, sun-dried hair.

"Hannah," I moaned. "That feels so good. Don't stop."

"Mmmm," Hannah hummed in assent.

I was enjoying Hannah's attention on my clit and could have come from that alone. But after a few minutes, she started caressing the sides of my labia, then she inserted two fingers inside my sopping hole. I groaned in pleasure, suddenly flashing back to the image of Emma getting eaten out by Bonnie on the log in the forest. I placed my hands beside Hannah's head and pulled her in closer to my throbbing snatch. When she began curling her two fingers against the inside of my pussy on my G-spot, I gasped out loud.

"Yes, Hannah!" I moaned. "Right there. Suck me. I'm going to come all over your pretty face. Make me cum, Han!"

Hannah moaned louder into my pussy and stepped up the pace of her licking and finger movements. I could feel my orgasm welling up inside me and I lifted my hips in preparation for the coming climax. When it poured over me, I couldn't stop screaming out in pleasure.

"Fuck, yes, Hannah! I'm coming, baby! I'm cumming in your sweet mouth. Ohhhh, I'm cumming so hard!"

Hannah held me tightly until I stopped twitching, then she lay back on the foot of my air mattress and scooted her hips up until our pussies were touching.

"Mmmm, Jade," she said. "Your pussy is so warm. I want to fuck you and feel your juices running all over me."

She tried rocking her hips awkwardly against me to create more friction, but I could tell she was getting frustrated trying to generate sustained and steady contact. After a couple of minutes of awkward flailing, I sat up on my air mattress and kneeled over her.

"Let me do this, hun," I said, looking into her eyes.

I placed my right thigh under one side of her hips then lifted my other leg over her stomach until we were in a sideways scissor position with me sitting on top. When I started rocking my hips and grinding our clits together, she gasped.

"*God*, yes! Fuck me, Jade! Fuck my aching pussy. I want to feel you cum all over me again."

"Fuck that," I said. "I want to feel you cum on me. It's your turn to lie back and enjoy my attention. Just focus on the pleasure—"

"Oh, oh, uhnnn!" Hannah panted. "Yes, Jade. That feels so good. Fuck me, honey, with your sweet cunt. Make me cum all over your sweet pussy!"

Hannah began flailing against the side of the tent as she screamed and moaned. I was certain that the whole campsite must have heard what was going on, but neither of us cared. We were so lost in the moment and enjoying our rising pleasure, we would have gladly fucked each other in full view of the other girls right now.

As I listened to Hannah's breathing grow more ragged and her moans increasing in volume, I wondered if Emma was playing with herself like I had yesterday listening to her. Hannah was rocking her hips wildly against me now and tearing at the sides of our tent. I knew she was close and I placed my hands around her hips and dug my nails into the sides of her ass as I pulled her harder against me.

"Now, Han!" I prompted her. "*Come* for me, baby. Let me feel you gush all over my gaping pussy!"

That was apparently all Hannah was waiting for, and she curled her body up toward me and held out her hand. I interlaced my fingers between hers and clasped her hand firmly. I could feel Hannah's grip growing progressively tighter until she finally grunted and exhaled loudly.

"Fuck! I'm *coming*, Jade! I'm cumming all over your sweet cunt. Fuck me, baby!"

I wanted to just focus on Hannah's pleasure and give her a full and proper fucking, but when she spoke those words I couldn't hold back any longer. As I came with her, we both sprayed our juices all over each other's pussies and thighs, screaming and moaning in delight. We shook and spasmed together for almost a full minute as we locked our cunts together in a paroxysm of pleasure.

When we finally collapsed beside each other on my air mattress, we heard the distinctive sound of girls' moaning coming from both of the other tents. We giggled and kissed each other listening to the other girls enjoying each other, then we made love for another hour before falling asleep in each other's arms in my sleeping bag.

4

———

GROUP FUN

The next morning, we all met around the campfire for hot chocolate. At first, we just made small talk about the scenery and how well everybody was sleeping with all the fresh air. Nobody wanted to broach the subject of what had obviously happened last night in each of our tents. As usual, Hannah was the first to break the awkward silence.

"Well, it's obvious that we were doing a lot more than just *sleeping* last night!"

We all looked at each other sheepishly and smiled.

"I think we should mix it up tonight," she said. "I propose that we change the bunking arrangements. You know, to make it more *interesting*. If we're gonna do this, we should at least *share the spoils*, shouldn't we?"

I glared at Hannah in mock indignation.

"*What?!*" I said. "You've grown *bored* with me already?"

Hannah leaned across our log and planted a big wet kiss on my lips.

"No baby," she said. "I could never grow tired of you. It's just that we only have a few more days out here and we're not going to have too many more chances like this. We can't fit *everybody* in one tent—"

"Hannah has a point," Lilly said, smiling at her partner, Madison. "It's obvious that we were all getting turned on listening to the others having fun. My panties haven't been dry since I heard Emma and Bonnie getting it on two nights ago."

"You *heard* us?!" Emma said. "Why didn't you say something?"

"I didn't want to put you on the spot. I wasn't sure if you guys wanted to share the love. But after last night, I think it's safe to say all bets are off."

We all looked at each other tentatively around the campfire.

"So...who goes with who?" I asked, sensing an argument over who got to sleep with Emma next. "Do we draw lots or something?"

"You make it sound like we're choosing who goes into battle!" Hannah joked. "Besides, we don't just have to stick with *one* partner, do we? We can always move around..."

"You mean play musical tents?" Maddie kidded.

"Something like that," Hannah said.

"I don't think there's any rules for this sort of thing," Lilly interjected. "Let's see how the chips fall. What do you say we work up our appetite a little bit with some more hiking and canoeing? Maybe we can find another waterfall to play in. That should get our juices flowing!"

We all looked at each other excitedly around the fire, contemplating what lay ahead for each of us. When my eyes met Emma's, we lingered a little longer, smiling as we fanned our legs together unconsciously.

"Right, then," Lilly said, reaching into the cooler. "Who's up for some more of that Canadian bacon?"

"I definitely could use a little *meat* right now," Hannah said, winking at me.

We spent the rest of the day swimming, fishing, and canoeing around the lake. When we found another waterfall, we took off our clothes and frolicked and washed ourselves in the warm fountain. We rubbed our naked bodies together playfully under the falling water, but nobody made any moves to go further. It seemed like everybody was saving themselves for the main event later this evening. But the few moments I had touching Emma's naked body were electrifying, and I knew that I wanted her all to myself if I could find a way to swing it.

When we got back to our camp, Lilly cleaned and cooked the fresh catch we'd caught that day, then we roasted some more marshmallows while we waited for the first one to make the initial move. Emma kept glancing in my direction, and after a half hour or so she motioned with her head toward the brush. I understood her meaning immediately and excused myself on the pretense of having to relieve myself.

"I think I hear the call of the wild," I said, picking up a roll of toilet paper and standing up off my log. "You girls don't go anywhere. We've still got the whole night ahead of us."

I headed into the bush to do my business, and a minute later Emma stood up and excused herself too. She headed in a different direction into the bush but quickly backtracked in my direction. We met on the fishing bank near the lily pond and giggled.

"Whew!" Emma said, smiling at me. "*That* was awkward. I thought we'd never find a chance to get away!"

"You've felt the same way?" I said, wondering if she felt as strongly toward me as I did toward her.

"Of course! I've been dying to get into your pants ever since the first day when we rode together in the back seat of the rental—."

I leaned in and kissed Emma hard on her lips. We pressed our bodies together and quickly fumbled to take our clothes off. We side-stepped awkwardly towards a tree and I pressed her against the trunk, then reached down and inserted two fingers into her sopping pussy. It wasn't very romantic, but I wanted to fuck her so bad. I pulled my palm up hard against her mound and began finger-fucking her roughly with my hand while I kissed her passionately.

As Emma panted I could hear the sound of her bare back rubbing against the bark of the tree. After a couple of minutes, she pulled away and looked at me.

"Do you mind if we head back to the camp and go into my tent? It's not very comfortable out here, and I'm getting eaten alive by the mosquitoes. Let's go somewhere cozier where we can take our time and do this right. I want to make love to you slowly and feel every part of you."

I looked into Emma's eyes and smiled. She didn't need to ask me twice. I'd been so wrapped up in my own lust, I hadn't noticed that I'd also been stung three times on my ass. We quickly pulled on our clothes and scampered back to the camp. When we got to the fire pit, all of the girls were gone. We looked around and noticed movement in two of the tents. Emma's was the only one that was still, so we unzipped the front and wiggled inside. We tore off each other's clothes then snuggled together into her sleeping bag to warm up from the evening chill.

At first, we just ran our hands over each other's bodies and held each other close trying to warm up in the soft bedroll, while we giggled like two little girls. But it didn't take long for things to heat up. I kissed Emma on her mouth and pressed my tongue between her lips while I ground my hips against hers. When I slipped my thigh between her legs and pressed my knee against her warm box, Emma moaned softly in my mouth. I was surprised how wet she was already. The inside of her thighs were coated with her slick lubrication all the way down to her knees.

I lifted myself up and looked at Emma's pretty face as she sighed from the feeling of my thigh sliding between her legs, then I lowered my face to her chest. I'd been dying to suck on her little breasts from the moment I saw her, and her nipples puckered inside my mouth as she pushed her body against me. I squeezed her tits with two hands as I moved from one breast to the other, savoring the taste of her sweet, tender nubs.

Emma reached down and cupped my breasts while I sucked on her, pinching and rolling my thick nipples between her fingers. I lifted myself up and rolled my tits across hers, feeling our erect nipples rubbing against one another. I could feel her hips rising and swaying in obvious need of attention, and I moved my head further down.

I nibbled on her soft pubis for a few moments, then I kissed my way across her abdomen onto the side of her ass, biting her playfully on her cheek. She turned her body to give me more access, and I gently flipped her over onto her stomach. I could see her magnificent ass in the moonlight, and I cupped and squeezed her buttock muscles, marveling at how perfectly round and tight they were. Then I spread her cheeks and thrust my mouth inside her crack.

Emma gasped when I found her rosebud and began

licking around her opening. I knew she was clean because I'd watched her wash herself in the waterfall and noticed that she hadn't gone into the woods since then. She tilted her ass upward and moaned loudly while I squeezed her ass and licked her anus. Then I spread her legs apart and thrust my hand between her legs.

The soft fabric of the sleeping bag was already soaked through from her wetness, and I easily slid my fingers into her slippery hole. As I flicked my tongue over her tender rosebud, I began to thrust my fingers in and out of her pussy. She grunted with each thrust and began wailing in pleasure as I pounded my hand into her.

"Oh! Oh! Oh! she growled, as her body slid forward and back over the air mattress. "Fuck me, Jade!" she said. "Suck my ass!"

I turned my hand over until my palm was facing down, then I slipped the rest of my fingers into her and began fucking her harder. I could feel Emma's pussy opening up inside and knew that she was close to coming. I curled my fingers and trilled her G-spot.

"Fuck, Jade!' she screamed. "Don't stop! Make me cum! I'm going to cum!"

Emma grunted like a wild animal as she pushed her hips down hard onto my hand and squeezed her thighs and buttocks muscles together, burying my face in her ass. I could feel her pussy and anus spasming in hard contractions as she grunted with each pulse. I held her for a few moments, then gently kissed her cheeks as she flopped down onto the air mattress.

A few minutes later, the zipper on the front of our tent opened and Hannah and Maddie stuck their heads through the flap.

"Do you guys want some company?" she said, smiling

like a Cheshire Cat. "It sounds like *somebody's* having all the fun in here."

Emma and I looked at one another and laughed.

"The more the merrier!" I said, motioning for them to come in. The girls scampered into our tent but just as Hannah began closing the zipper, Lilly stuck her head in.

"Feel like two more?" she asked.

We all giggled as everybody piled into our tent, and soon after we formed a giant swirling mass of bodies, sucking, licking, and tribbing each other into the wee hours of the night.

We fell asleep on top of one another around four a.m. It wasn't until almost midday the next morning when we slowly crawled out of the tent. While Lilly prepared brunch, the rest of us went our separate ways into the bush to relieve ourselves. A few minutes later, Hannah called out from the north side of the island. We all rushed to her thinking she'd fallen or hurt herself, then we saw her crouched down, pointing over the lake.

"Look," she said. "Do you see that?"

I squinted into the distance and saw a canoe with two occupants slowly paddling across the lake, on a parallel course with our island.

"I guess we're not the only ones out here, after all," I said, nodding.

"Can you make out who it is?" Bonnie said. "I mean, are they boys or girls—or one of each? Should we invite them over to share brunch?"

We all looked at each other, hesitating. None of us was

sure we were ready to share ourselves with anyone else after last night's orgy.

Hannah suddenly looked in my direction.

"Jade," she said. "Did you bring your binoculars from home? Let's see what they look like close-up. If it's a couple, they might just want to be left alone."

I nodded and hurried back to my tent to retrieve my field glasses from my backpack. When I returned to the group, Hannah took the glasses from my hand as we all crouched down on the mossy ground, spying on the interlopers.

Hannah held the glasses up to her eyes and swiveled the focus button on top.

"Holy shit!" she said. "It's two *guys*. Two very *young* guys!"

"*How* young exactly?" Lilly said.

Hannah paused as she steadied the binoculars over her forehead and adjusted the focus.

"Late teens, early twenties at most. And they're cute! Long hair, a little rough around the edges maybe, but buff!"

"I guess we know at least *one* of us is on board with that," I said.

We all peered over at Lilly and she chuckled as she smiled at us slyly.

"Sounds like the kind of guys who would drive a beat-up Pathfinder," she said, remembering the other car in the parking lot of our trailhead.

Hannah turned around and looked at each of us carefully.

"What do you say, girls? Should we invite them over? I mean, I don't want to spoil our fun, but this could mix things up quite nicely. Think of all the *permutations* this could make. I bet those horny teenagers would jump at a chance to join six sexy girls alone on a deserted island."

We all looked at one another for a moment, then we giggled and stood up on the bank of our island.

"Over here!" Hannah yelled, waving her arms over her head trying to get the attention of the two paddlers. "Come to Momma, you sexy little hunks."

We all jumped up and down on the shore screaming and yelling, and the canoeists stopped paddling for a moment, looking in our direction. Then they looked at one another, unsure of our intention.

"Oh, for crying out loud," Hannah said, peeling off her shirt and bra. "I think they need a little more encouragement."

We all peeled off our tops and jumped up and down on the shoreline, our tits bouncing up and down.

"Here we are!" Lilly shouted. "Six sexy, horny girls! Come dip your paddles in some even hotter water!"

The canoeists suddenly began paddling again, and I saw the boat begin to turn in our direction.

Oh boy, I thought. *Now we've really gotten ourselves into a row of trouble...*

Some habits are harder to break than others...

Artificial intelligence never felt so real...

THE PERSONAL TRAINER

AN EROTIC ADVENTURE

VICTORIA RUSH

Feeling the burn never felt so good...

Books 6 - 10 in the bestselling series - now 60% off.

WET DREAM - PREVIEW
RUBBING ONE OUT

I fell asleep that night with visions of futa girls crawling over my body as I sucked, fucked, and played with their ladydicks all night long. It didn't take long for my dreams to turn in this direction, and within minutes I was transported to an ancient Arabian kingdom filled with sorcerers and villains. I dreamt that I was the daughter of a powerful emir, betrothed to the king's son. But I wasn't ready to be married yet, not least because I was secretly carrying on an affair with his pretty daughter Farah.

Farah and I had tried to run away, but she was caught by the palace guards while I escaped to a remote cave in the Arabian desert. After a few days without food and water, I began to explore the large cavern in search of nourishment. I came upon a grotto illuminated by a beam of sunlight shining from a crack in the ceiling. The ray projected onto a gleaming pile of jewels and glazed pottery, sitting beside a gurgling pool of water.

I stumbled toward the pool and began guzzling up the liquid into my parched lips. After I recharged my dehydrated body, I began to sift through the trove. It had obviously been placed to hide someone's riches in a location with an abundant source of hydration. Its keepers would have to travel a long distance over the desert to get here. Surely, they'd have also stored some extra *food* provisions to tide them over on their long journey?

I began to tear off the lids of the assorted containers, desperately looking for anything to eat. The pots and bowls clattered against one another, occasionally breaking into shards, but preserving the integrity of the pretty porcelain-ware was the last thing on my mind. To my dismay, the bowls were only filled with more jewels and coins. The cave probably carried a king's ransom worth of treasure, but that would be of little help to me if I died of starvation in the next few days.

I continued rummaging through the pile until I came upon an odd-shaped jar with a small hole at the top of its tapered end. I picked up the vessel and it was heavier than I expected, which meant it had to be filled with something. The lid to the jar was sealed, so I shook the container to discern its contents. It made a strange rustling sound, suggesting there was something soft inside.

Could it be a grain or nut storage jar? I thought.

I stuck my finger through the hole to see if I could feel what it was, but the contents kept moving around, almost like there was something *alive* inside. I peered through the hole, but there wasn't enough light in the cave to see beyond the curved flute at its end. Thinking it might be a small mouse or some other creature, I banged the vessel against a nearby rock in an attempt to break it open. At this point, I was so hungry I could have eaten just about anything.

But unlike all the other delicate pots and bowls, this vessel wouldn't break. I held the container up into the light to try to read the inscription on its flanks. There had to be something valuable in this flask for it to be fortified so strongly, I thought. The container had a thick coating of soot, so I rubbed my sleeve on its side. Suddenly, I heard a strange rumbling coming from inside the flask as a tendril of smoke began to rise from the hole.

The discharge grew thicker and heavier, and the container began to shake violently in my hands. I looked up at the smoke filling the chamber and gasped as it began to take the shape of a man. He was wearing a large turban and embroidered tunic over puffy trousers. On his feet he wore bejeweled jester slippers. When the apparition began to speak, I almost fainted.

"What is so important," the ghost thundered, "that you've shaken Suleiman the Great from his slumber?"

"I'm sorry..." I stammered, in equal parts frightened and mesmerized by the impressive figure. "I didn't know what was inside..."

"Well, you've awoken the jinni now. What is it that you desire?"

"Jinni?" I said, my eyes widening in wonder. "You mean *genie*? Are you some kind of genie?"

I glanced down at the vessel in my hands and realized it was an oil lamp.

"Are you the genie from Aladdin's Lamp?!" I exclaimed, suddenly excited by my find.

"I don't know who this Aladdin is," the ghost said, "but as the bearer of the lamp, I am beholden to only you. What is it that you wish?"

"You mean you can grant me a *wish*?! Just like in the famous story from Arabian Nights?"

"Yes," the genie said. "*Three* wishes, in fact. So choose wisely. I will return to my cozy home after I've granted your wishes and will not come out again for a hundred years."

"Oh boy!" I said, not hesitating to give it much thought. There was only one thing on my mind right now, and that was my grumbling stomach. "I need food. Lots of food. Enough sustenance to carry me back over the desert to the sultan's palace."

"Your wish is my command," the genie said, raising his arms then snapping his fingers toward the ground beside me.

Suddenly, I was surrounded by piles of fruit, nuts, and dried meat. I grabbed a handful of lamb and rammed it into my mouth, gobbling it down in chunks. As I felt the energy returning to my body, I looked back up at the genie.

"Choose wisely, young lady," he said. "You only have two wishes remaining. That food won't last very long. You might want to ask for something you can enjoy for the rest of your days."

I looked at the genie and paused. I was already surrounded by all the jewels and wealth I could ever possibly need. What else could I use that would bring me additional enjoyment? As I began to feel the nourishment coursing through my veins and reinvigorating my organs, I suddenly smiled.

"I'd like to have a man's cock," I said. "But not just any cock. I want a long, thick one. One that I can cum with repeatedly whenever I want."

"Your wish is my command," the genie said, raising his arms, preparing to deliver my request.

"Wait!" I shouted. "But don't want you to take away my lady parts. I still want to look like a woman, with normal breasts and a pussy and a clit. I just also want to have a fully functioning penis."

The genie paused for a moment as he considered my request.

"I suppose that still counts as one wish," he said. "Not taking anything else away doesn't require any extra effort. Do you have any *other* special requirements for this man penis you dream of?"

Hmm, I thought. *I should be careful he doesn't just give me any old dick.*

I thought about the ones that I'd particularly enjoyed over the years. Then I held up my hand and separated my fingers a few inches.

"I want it to be circumcised," I said. "And straight. Let's say eight inches long, and...*two* inches thick. And nicely upstanding when it's erect. A forty-five-degree angle against my abdomen sounds about right."

"Done."

The genie raised his arms again then flung his hands in my direction. At first, I didn't feel anything, but when I lifted my skirt, I gasped. I had a magnificent, golden-brown, circumcised manhose hanging between my legs! I spread my thighs apart and began to fiddle with my new joystick, and it immediately began to fatten and lengthen. As the phallus began to rise up between my legs, I felt a new kind of tingling between my legs. I watched transfixed as my new member jerked and rose with each new pulse of my heart.

I finally had my very own cock! I thought. *My very own throbbing, bobbing, hard cock!*

I couldn't wait to play with it as I circled my fingers around the shaft and squeezed the hard meat in my hand.

"Um," the genie said, peering at me as I sat dumbfoundedly with my fist around my hard-on. "What would you like for your final wish? I'd like to get back to my peaceful slumber sometime today, if you don't mind."

"Oh, yeah," I said, pausing to contemplate what else I could possibly want.

For a moment, I considered asking him for a playmate, a pretty girl that I could use my new cock on right away. But then I remembered Farah, and I had a better idea. If I was ever going to sneak back into the palace and steal her away, I'd need a pretty good disguise.

"I want you to change my looks a little bit. Just enough so people won't recognize me when they see me. But I still want to look feminine, around my same age, and pretty."

"Your final wish is my command!" the genie said, as he flung his arms in the air then back toward me.

A cloud of smoke rose from my perch in the cave, and I peered over to look in the pool of water to see my reflection. A pretty brunette looked back at me, and I smiled.

This will do just fine, I thought.

Suddenly it occurred to me that I'd need additional resources to steal my beloved Farah away from the clutches of her powerful father.

"Wait!" I called out to the genie. "There's one more thing!"

"I'm sorry," the genie said as he began to shrink and vaporize in the cool cavern air. "You've used up all of your allotted wishes. I wish you well. Now please do me a favor and hide my little lamp so I won't be disturbed for another hundred years."

The smoky apparition began to shrink and collapse, then the swirling cloud of smoke disappeared back into the container. I looked around the cave for a safe place to deposit the lamp, then I pushed a large boulder aside and placed the lamp in a recession behind the rock. If I couldn't use the genie's power for another hundred years, then at least I'd be able to pass it along to my family where I'd hidden him.

As I walked back to the pool of water, I glanced at my

reflection once again. It was strange to see someone other than myself looking back at me, and I ran my hands over my face to be sure it was really me. The girl looking back at me was beautiful with big doe-eyes, high cheekbones, and full pouty lips. As I smiled at my reflection, my penis suddenly started rising up between my legs again.

Apparently, my newly installed manhood *also* found the girl in the water attractive! I pulled off my dress and under-clothes and appraised my full body in the mirrored reflection. I still had nice full, firm breasts and round, shapely hips. I spread my legs and pulled my skin apart. And I still had a pussy—*thank you, Genie!*

I placed my hand over my slit and traced my middle finger up toward the junction of my lips to make sure I still had my clit. As I began to circle it in my familiar way, my eyes widened as my new cock swelled and hardened, and rose in a series of sexy pulsing bobs until it pointed straight up at a forty-five-degree angle.

The genie was true to his word. My cock was truly magnificent. Long, firm, and thick, with a large plum-shaped bulbous head that was already leaking sticky fluid out of its slit. I placed my finger over the opening and swirled it over the viscous fluid, then raised my finger to my mouth.

A little salty—but not disagreeable, I thought.

I couldn't wait to see my cum shoot out of my dick when I had a full orgasm. I placed my fist awkwardly around the shaft and began jerking it like I'd seen so many men do before. I was glued to my reflection as I watched myself masturbate my big cock over the pool. Even though I could feel the pleasurable sensations emanating from my crotch, it still felt like I was watching an entirely different person.

But the feeling coming from my man dick was undeniable. It wasn't all that different from the sensations I felt when I played with my pussy and clit, but it was still...*different*. It felt—*bigger*. I began moaning and grunting as I whacked my big cock, recognizing the pleasure rising up within me, emanating from my hips.

The more I rubbed it, the deeper shade of purple my cock became. The head of my cock was now glistening with a thick coat of sticky translucent fluid. When I placed my hand around the bulb and began to massage the lubrication into my skin, I threw my head back and groaned.

So that's where all the action is, I murmured.

The head of a man's cock was a lot more sensitive than the rest of his organ, just like a woman's clit. All the super-sensitive nerve endings were concentrated in the end. I grasped the base of my organ with my left hand and placed my right hand over the upper half and began jerking myself with two hands.

The feeling emanating from my groin was indescribable. I was just starting to get the hang of this whole jerking off thing, and *two* hands was definitely better than one! As I humped my hips into my hands watching the head of my wet cock pumping in and out of the end of my fist, the strange reflection in the pool peered back at me. As I watched her pretty mouth open in ecstasy, I pounded my cock hard against my mound and moaned in delirious pleasure.

As I began to feel the familiar feeling of an orgasm welling up inside me, I refocused my attention on the tip of my cock as it pistoned in and out of my hands. I didn't want to miss this fireworks show for all the money in the world!

I grunted and groaned as I thrashed my head from side to side, barely able to stand up from the pleasure consuming me. Suddenly, I felt a different kind of sensation, as if I had to pee. Coming from deep inside my perineum, I could feel something pushing to come out. As the crest of my orgasm hit me, I screamed out loud, echoing throughout the grotto.

"Yes!" I screamed. "I'm cumming! I'm cumming from my big, manly cock! Fuck! I'm cummmingggg!"

Suddenly, a thick string of white fluid spurted out the tip of my cock as my pole pulsed repeatedly in my hands. I gasped with each contraction, as a new spurt of white goo squirted out of my joystick, making ripples in the water below. I squeezed my cock so hard between my two hands, I was afraid I might break it. But it just kept throbbing and pulsing in my hands, until the last few spurts of come dribbled from the head. When I finally finished coming, I hunched over, exhausted from the experience of having my first ladyboy orgasm.

That wouldn't be the last of my big dick orgasms today. As the shaft of overhead sunlight drew a wide arc across the wall of my cave, I had five more orgasms before falling fast asleep on my heaping pile of treasure.

But I was more pleased that I'd found a *different* kind of treasure today—the kind that only *I* could spend.

Read More

ABOUT THE AUTHOR

If you would like to receive notification of new book(s) in Jade's Erotic Adventures, follow me at http://bookbub.com/authors/victoria-rush.

If you have a moment, please post a brief review on my Amazon book page at mybook.to/gc . Even just a couple of sentences will help other readers find and enjoy this book as much as you hopefully did.

Follow, share, like, and comment at:

www.facebook.com/authorvictoriarush
www.pinterest.com/authorvictoriarush
www.twitter.com/authorvictoriarush
authorvictoriarush@outlook.com

Hope to see you again soon!